Acting Edition

How The Light Gets In

by E. M. Lewis

I0591767

ⅠSAMUEL FRENCHⅠ

ISBN 978-0-573-70991-3

www.concordtheatricals.com
www.concordtheatricals.co.uk

FOR PRODUCTION INQUIRIES

UNITED STATES AND CANADA
info@concordtheatricals.com
1-866-979-0447

UNITED KINGDOM AND EUROPE
licensing@concordtheatricals.co.uk
020-7054-7298

Each title is subject to availability from Concord Theatricals Corp.,
depending upon country of performance. Please be aware that *HOW
THE LIGHT GETS IN* may not be licensed by Concord Theatricals
Corp. in your territory. Professional and amateur producers should
contact the nearest Concord Theatricals Corp. office or licensing
partner to verify availability.

This work is published by Samuel French, an imprint of Concord
Theatricals Corp.

How The Light Gets In was developed at Boston Court Pasadena in its New Play Festival and at Chatauqua Theater Company. The play had its world premiere at Boston Court Pasadena in 2019 with Jessica Kubzansky as Artistic Director. The production was directed by Emilie Pascale Beck, Scenic Designer Tesshi Nakagawa, Costume Designer Ann Closs-Farley, Lighting Designer Sarah Resch, Sound Designer Jack Arky, Properties Designer Jenny Smith Cohn & Jess Soto, Assistant Director Dyoni Isom, Casting Director Julia Flores, Production Stage Manager Trixie Eunhae Hong. The cast was as follows:

GRACE WHEELER . . . . Amy Sloan
HARUKI SAKAMOTO . . . . Ryun Yu
KAT LANE . . . . Chelsea Kurtz
TOMMY Z . . . . Dieterich Gray

How The Light Gets In received the 2020 Harold and Mimi Steinberg New Play Award from the American Theater Critics Association.

CHARACTERS

GRACE WHEELER – (F/46) – A travel writer who has never been anywhere. She volunteers as a docent at the Japanese Garden (but she isn't Japanese).

HARUKI SAKAMOTO – (M/52) – An architect who specializes in creating buildings set in natural spaces. Japanese.

KAT LANE – (F/17) – A young runaway. She wears lots of layers of clothes that obscure her gender. Hollow-eyed and wary.

TOMMY Z – (M/39) – A tattoo artist. Rough and dangerous-looking at first glance, but big-hearted. Has a special gift of seeing a person clearly, and drawing just the right thing on their skin.

SETTING

A clean, open space that will become all the locations in the play – a hospital, Grace's house, a tattoo parlor, a highway overpass.

A wooden bench, set under the graceful drape of a weeping willow tree's branches in the Japanese Garden, is the only thing that stays in the space throughout.

Light and sound will carry us everywhere we need to go.

TIME

Present day.

AUTHOR'S NOTES

The actors playing Kat and Tommy Z will also play a variety of other characters, as indicated.

*(When the lights come up, **GRACE**, **HARUKI**, **TOMMY Z** and **KAT** are all on stage.)*

*(**KAT** and **TOMMY** look out at the audience for a moment. **KAT** turns to **TOMMY**, who gives her an encouraging look. She takes a deep breath.)*

KAT. Once upon a time...

TOMMY Z. Once upon a time? Really?

KAT. All my favorite stories start that way! Stories about handsome princes and fairy godmothers and dragons and witches and wolves.

TOMMY Z. This isn't a fairy tale.

KAT. This is a story about a girl who is lost in the woods, and the people who find her.

> *(**TOMMY** shakes his head, unconvinced. Then he offers a completely new beginning, with a classic comic book flair.)*

TOMMY Z. In a dark time, in a dark place, when the world has fallen into death and chaos, we meet a superhero who has lost his powers.

> *(**KAT** shakes her head, no.)*

KAT. This isn't a story about death and chaos!

TOMMY Z. Are you sure?

KAT. *(Determined.)* This is a love story.

TOMMY Z. A love story?!

(**KAT** *looks out at the audience for a moment, including them.*)

KAT. This is a story about Grace Wheeler, a travel writer who has never been anywhere.

TOMMY Z. And Haruki Sakamoto, a famous architect who can't figure out how to design a simple tea house.

(*The light shifts, and suddenly, we are in the Japanese Garden.*)

(**KAT** *looks around, appreciating the lush, green peacefulness for a moment.*)

KAT. The story begins here. In the Japanese Garden. Where Grace volunteers as a docent.

(**KAT** *and* **TOMMY** *give way as* **GRACE** *steps forward, into her docent self, speaking to the audience, as if they're all on the tour she's been leading.*)

GRACE. Watch your step! The natural stone pathways can be dangerous, if you're not careful.

(*Beat.*)

Everything here was made to help the visitor slow down, and pay attention. Your reward is the beauty you see in every corner, from the Raked Garden and the Small Koi Bridge to the Moss Temple and the Ishidoro, or Old Stone Lantern.

(**GRACE** *steps to one side.*)

That brings us to the end of our tour! Thank you for joining us here at the Japanese Garden. Don't forget to visit the gift shop before you go!

(*Beat.*)

One last look! And then | Step gently into the loud | and perilous world.

(**KAT** *moves over toward the weeping willow tree as she says...*)

KAT. On a rainy Thursday, just after she's given a tour of the garden, Grace's cell phone buzzes in her pocket.

(**KAT** *ducks beneath the fronds of the weeping willow tree in the garden, and disappears from sight.*)

TOMMY Z. Bzzz... bzzz... bzzz...

(**GRACE**'*s face changes instantly, as wary now as she was friendly a moment ago.*)

(*She's been waiting for this call.*)

(**GRACE** *takes the phone out of her pocket, and then hits accept, and puts the phone to her ear.*)

GRACE. Hello...

(*She listens.*)

Hi. Yes, I've been... I've been waiting for your call.

(*She listens. And there is suddenly a terrible stillness about her.*)

Okay.

(*Pause.*)

Okay.

(*Pause.*)

Okay.

(*She listens.*)

Okay.

(Pause.)

What happens now?

(She listens, nodding occasionally.)

*(Behind **GRACE**, the dangling branches of the weeping willow tree part as **KAT** looks out at her.)*

Okay. Nine o'clock Tuesday.

*(**GRACE** ends the call.)*

(A moment.)

(Then she sits down hard on the bench behind her, like her strings have been cut. Her face is blank.)

*(**KAT** peers out from the willow tree branches, looking at **GRACE**... then steps out from her hiding place, and finds her voice.)*

KAT. Are you okay?

*(**GRACE** turns and looks up at **KAT**.)*

Because you don't look okay.

(A long moment.)

Did someone tell you something bad?

(A moment.)

*(Then **GRACE** nods.)*

I'm sorry.

*(**GRACE** musters up a smile.)*

GRACE. Thank you.

(Pause.)

I'm okay.

KAT. Okay.

(A long moment.)

You're my favorite talker, of all the talkers.

GRACE. I am?

(Beat; gently.)

We're called 'docents.'

KAT. You have a really pretty way of saying things.

GRACE. Thank you.

KAT. "Step gently into..."

GRACE. The loud and perilous world.

(A moment.)

That's a haiku.

KAT. What's a haiku?

GRACE. It's a kind of poem that –

(Beat.)

Where did you come from?

*(After a reluctant moment, **KAT** points at the weeping willow tree.)*

That's a tree.

*(**KAT** nods.)*

You were hiding under the tree?

*(**KAT** nods.)*

For how long?

KAT. Two months.

GRACE. Two months?!

    (Beat.)

You've been living here, under the weeping willow tree for two months?

KAT. Is that what you call it?

GRACE. Yes. That's what we call it. Because the branches...

    *(**GRACE** ruffles her fingers through the air, and we hear the sound of water – perhaps from a rain stick – gently falling.)*

KAT. Don't tell anybody.

    *(**GRACE** nods.)*

GRACE. Two months?

KAT. Not steady. Just sometimes. When I can.

    (Beat.)

They fixed the fence, so I had to figure out another way in.

GRACE. Now how do you get in?

KAT. I climb down the rocks from the park, over by the waterfall.

    *(**TOMMY Z** gestures toward **KAT** and **GRACE**.)*

TOMMY Z. Grace doesn't tell anyone that Kat is living under the weeping willow tree.

KAT. Which Kat appreciates.

TOMMY Z. She brings Kat homemade soup in little Tupperware containers.

KAT. Which Kat also appreciates.

TOMMY Z. They sit on the bench, in the garden, and talk about things.

> *(**GRACE** makes room for **KAT** on the bench. She pulls two little Tupperware containers of homemade soup out of her bag, and offers one to **KAT**, who opens it immediately and begins to eat. **GRACE** sets hers on the bench beside her.)*

GRACE. Do you have a family?

> *(**KAT** doesn't answer.)*

Should I not have asked that?

KAT. It's okay.

> *(But she still doesn't answer.)*

GRACE. Do you go to school?

KAT. No.

GRACE. Why not?

> *(**KAT** doesn't answer.)*

How long have you been on your own?

KAT. A while.

> *(Pause.)*

I don't want to talk about me anymore.

> *(**GRACE** nods.)*

Why are you here?

GRACE. The director of the Garden hired me to write their new marketing brochure. They had this sweet little lady who didn't know anything about marketing, who had been doing all their marketing. And she was there at my meeting with the director, glaring at me through her little glasses.

    (Beat.)

She'd proposed this ridiculous line for their promotional materials.

SWEET LITTLE LADY. *(Voiced by* **TOMMY Z***.)* You'll find what you need at the Japanese Garden.

GRACE. Who would write that? I'd never write that.

    (Beat.)

But that night... that night I woke up, in the middle of the night, I woke up, and thought... "What if it's true?!"

    (Beat.)

I signed up to be a docent the next day.

TOMMY Z. The two of them talk about all sorts of things. But it takes a while before Grace tells Kat what that phone call was about. Even though she can't think about anything else. And can't sleep at night.

    (Beat.)

It's really hard to tell people really true things.

    *(***KAT** *nods.)*

    *(***GRACE** *stands up, and steps away from the bench.)*

    *(***KAT** *continues to sit there, listening.)*

    (Listening.)

GRACE. Ever since the... since the doctor told me the results of the biopsy... I've had the urge to touch my breast. Cradle it in my hand. Before they...

(Pause.)

This is really hard.

(Pause.)

It hurts a little. Ever since the biopsy. You know what a biopsy is? How they do it?

(KAT shakes her head, no.)

They make you lie down on a table and they put your breast in a vise and squeeze it, then they use a long needle to –

(GRACE makes a violent drilling motion with her hands, which is accompanied by the sound of a jackhammer.)

– take samples from the area where they think there's something wrong. Then they put in a titanium clip, to mark the place, so they can find it again later, if they need to. A tiny titanium clip.

(A moment.)

I'm scaring you.

(KAT shakes her head, no, even though GRACE IS scaring her.)

(GRACE unbuttons the two top buttons of her blouse, and looks down at herself.)

It looks perfect. Except for the little scab where the biopsy needle went in. It looks perfectly perfect. Not super model perfect. Regular person perfect.

(Pause.)

If I was in a terrible accident and was all bloody and mangled by the side of the road and they scooped me up and took me to the hospital and were trying to sew me back together, <u>that</u> would be one thing. It would all be so fast, and I wouldn't have any choice. They would be saving me.

 (Beat.)

It's hard to look at my own perfect breast, regular person perfect breast, and imagine letting them take a knife to it and think of that as saving me.

 *(**KAT** nods.)*

TOMMY Z. Grace didn't really tell Kat all that. She's a little girl.

KAT. A young woman.

TOMMY Z. Really young.

 (Beat.)

What she really says is –

GRACE. That phone call? That I got?

 (Beat.)

Was me finding out that I have breast cancer.

 *(**KAT** nods.)*

TOMMY Z. It takes much longer for Kat to tell Grace why she's living under the weeping willow tree in the Japanese Garden.

KAT. When I turned eleven... I can't tell you what happened, what happened, what happened and then kept happening until – It was Thursday. I was supposed to be at school, but I wasn't at school. I was home alone, but I wasn't alone. I can't tell you who was there, I can't tell you anything, don't ask me to tell you, I can't ever go back...

TOMMY Z. Kat didn't really tell Grace all that. What she says is –

KAT. Home isn't safe.

(**GRACE** *nods.*)

(*To* **TOMMY.**)

It's really hard to tell people really true things.

(**TOMMY Z** *nods.*)

(*The light shifts, and suddenly we're in* **TOMMY Z**'s *tattoo parlor.*)

(**TOMMY Z** *gestures toward* **KAT.**)

TOMMY Z. She showed up at my door one day like a little... well... cat. The scared-ness and the hunger warring with each other. Months after I met her at the hospital. She just stood there in the doorway, looking at me. And I didn't move. And she said...

KAT. You told me I could come here.

TOMMY Z. And I said, "Yes." And then she disappeared.

(*A moment.*)

She came back four days later, and said...

KAT. You gave me your address and said you'd help me if I came here.

TOMMY Z. And I said, "Yes." And then she disappeared.

(*A moment.*)

She came back five days later and said...

KAT. I like your wall.

TOMMY Z. Thank you.

(Pause.)

When I bought the building, it hadn't been anything for, like, forty years. One wall was all messed up, where somebody drove through it. It was just brick and dirt and concrete and broken windows and old needles. You know?

*(**KAT** nods.)*

I got it for a pretty good price. And I knocked out the whole wall that was messed up.

And I found – over about a year, I found all these windows, and I pieced them together to make a new wall.

(Beat.)

In the morning, when the sun is coming up, it's like... a patchwork quilt of light.

*(**KAT** nods.)*

There's a little bag of cookies there by the door, if you want them.

(Beat.)

She grabbed them and disappeared.

(A moment.)

The seventh time she came, I had a stack of comic books and manga set out for her. And more cookies. And she sat down on the floor, right by the door, and stayed all day, eating cookies and watching me work and reading. *Batman* and *Fullmetal Alchemist* and *X-Men* and *Black Panther* and *Akira*. All the ones my brother Eddie and I have read forever.

(A moment.)

The eleventh time she came, she let me tattoo her wrists.

(*Beat.*)

I sat on the floor to make her feel safer. But it was really hard to do a good job, because she never stopped trembling.

(**TOMMY** *sits on the floor, and takes* **KAT***'s wrists gently in his hands.*)

KAT. What are you going to draw?

TOMMY Z. I don't know yet. First I gotta know your story.

(*A moment.*)

(*To the audience.*) And she stayed.

(*Beat.*)

And she told me.

(**KAT** *looks at her wrists, then at* **TOMMY Z.** *Then she returns to* **GRACE** *in the garden.*)

In the normal course of events, Kat and Grace would never meet, much less become friends.

KAT. But they do meet. And recognize something –

TOMMY Z. – something –

KAT. – in each other –

TOMMY Z. – in each other.

KAT. For completely different reasons, neither Kat nor Grace feels safe.

(*Pause.*)

They are not alone.

(*A moment.*)

TOMMY Z. Things move very fast for Grace after she receives her diagnosis.

KAT. She continues to work –

TOMMY Z. – as you do.

KAT. She meets with lots of doctors.

>   (**GRACE** *turns to* **KAT.**)

GRACE. Nobody asked what I do.

>   (*Beat.*)

Like it didn't matter.

>   (*Pause.*)

I'm a thing now.

KAT. You're not a thing.

>   (*Beat; searches for what to say.*)

You're a person.

>   (*Pause.*)

What <u>do</u> you do?

GRACE. I'm a travel writer.

KAT. That's a job?

GRACE. (*Amused.*) Yes, it's a job.

KAT. What do you actually...

>   (**KAT** *waves her hand around.*)

GRACE. Do?

>   (**KAT** *nods.*)

Write about amazing places, all over the world, in eight hundred words or less. Sometimes four hundred. People have very short attention spans.

KAT. What's the most amazing place you've ever been to?

GRACE. Oh, I don't go places. I just write about them.

KAT. How do you write about them if you don't go there?

GRACE. Research and imagination.

KAT. *(Beat.)* Oh...

(**KAT** *isn't sure what to make of that.*)

GRACE. It's not that I couldn't go places. I could have gone places all this time. It's just that...

(Beat.)

I didn't.

(A moment.)

TOMMY Z. Grace meets with the medical oncologist. The radiation oncologist. And finally –

KAT. – on a Wednesday –

TOMMY Z. – the surgical oncologist. Who explains what's going to happen next.

(A moment.)

She finds it kind of hard to lead her tour of the Japanese Garden that day.

(A moment.)

KAT. Haruki Sakamoto is also in the garden that day.

TOMMY Z. He's an architect from Japan who was commissioned to design a special tea house right here, in this spot.

> (**HARUKI** *balls up three drawings in a row from his drawing pad, and throws them on the ground in disgust.*)

KAT. He's been here for seven weeks.

TOMMY Z. He's taking forever to figure out how to do it. But nobody wants to say anything, because he's famous.

> (**HARUKI** *steps forward.*)

HARUKI. When I arrived here, I had no worries about this project. This is what I do. I design buildings! And it's not a large job. They don't want a large tea house. They don't have room for a large tea house. Easy, I thought!

> (**HARUKI** *gives a look, instantly realizing his mistake.*)

You laugh. Yes! So did the universe. It listens for such declarations.

> (**HARUKI** *gestures at the garden.*)

They held a formal welcome event for me here, with the big donors, when I arrived, very nice, only the best cheeses.

And after it has been going on for a while, and I have shaken all the right hands and sampled all the cheeses, I come out here to take a breath. And one of the men, who is here only for his wife, a man who carries his wealth in his belly like this...

> (**HARUKI** *bends his knees, and settles his weight back a little, like a heavy and confident man, as he and* **TOMMY Z**, *as the* **BIG MAN**, *sit down on the bench.*)

...he is here, smoking a cigar, and he offers me a cigar. And sometimes I like a cigar with another man, it's a good ritual. So we sit down on this bench, and smoke, and he asks me –

BIG MAN. *(Voiced by* **TOMMY Z.***)* Do you know what you're going to build here yet?

HARUKI. And I say no, not yet. And he says –

BIG MAN. Well, it shouldn't be hard. All you have to do is make something better than a bench under a tree.

> *(A moment.)*

HARUKI. And I sat there with him, smoking my cigar, the smoke drifting up into the blue sky that was slowly turning black and punctuating itself with stars, and I was instantly paralyzed.

> *(Beat.)*

Because what mortal could make something more beautiful than this?

> *(A moment.)*

KAT. The Japanese Garden has been closed for several hours when Grace lets herself in.

> *(***GRACE*** *steps around the side of the bench, picking up crumpled papers, and is surprised to see* **HARUKI** *sitting there.)*

GRACE. Oh! Hi! How are you?

HARUKI. *(Forcefully.)* Terrible!

> *(***GRACE*** *lets out a surprised laugh.)*

And you think this is funny?

GRACE. No! I just... It's always surprising to get a real answer to a rhetorical question.

HARUKI. It is after the hours. You are not supposed to be here.

GRACE. Neither are you.

HARUKI. I am an artist. We make our own rules.

GRACE. I'm a docent.

>   *(Beat.)*

Which usually means we make everybody follow the rules.

>   *(Beat.)*

But sometimes we go rogue.

HARUKI. You are going rogue?

GRACE. Don't I look like a person who is capable of going rogue?

>   *(**HARUKI** looks at **GRACE** doubtfully.)*

Looks can be deceiving.

HARUKI. I am trying to work.

GRACE. It looks like you're just sitting there.

HARUKI. Looks can be deceiving.

>   *(Pause.)*

What brings you here, in the night?

GRACE. I was feeling really... really...

>   *(Beat.)*

It's peaceful here.

HARUKI. You are not a peaceful person?

GRACE. Not right now.

>   *(Beat.)*

I keep crying on sidewalks. Suddenly, without any warning. Like a squall.

HARUKI. "Squall?"

GRACE. A sudden little storm out of nowhere.

HARUKI. Squall.

GRACE. It's the perfect word. I love finding the perfect word for things. It makes me so happy. A flush of happiness. Right up through me. I'm a writer. When I'm not being a docent. Travel writing is my real job. I'm just a docent here because...

HARUKI. It's peaceful.

GRACE. Yes.

HARUKI. What is upsetting you?

> (**GRACE** *makes a small keening sound as the tears well up without warning.*)

GRACE. Sorry!

HARUKI. Sorry!

> (**GRACE**'s *tears go on for a moment, with* **HARUKI** *not unsympathetic, but not sure what to do. Finally, he pulls a big white handkerchief out of his pocket and hands it to* **GRACE**. *She takes it and wipes her eyes.*)

GRACE. It keeps happening.

> (**HARUKI** *nods.*)

You know what I really need right now?

> *(Beat.)*

Someone to hold me.

HARUKI. *(Beat.)* I'm Japanese.

(GRACE laughs.)

Perhaps I could just nod at you gravely but sympathetically from over here.

GRACE. Has anybody ever told you you're really funny?

HARUKI. Never in my whole life.

(GRACE laughs again.)

GRACE. I'm Grace.

(She holds out her hand. HARUKI shakes it.)

HARUKI. Haruki.

GRACE. You're designing the new tea house.

HARUKI. I am trying.

(Beat.) You work here, yes? I've seen you.

GRACE. I volunteer two days a week. As a docent.

HARUKI. Hm.

GRACE. *(Beat.)* Hm, what?

(HARUKI doesn't answer.)

You don't have to be Japanese to work at the Japanese Garden.

HARUKI. It helps.

(A moment.)

TOMMY Z. The second time that Grace and Haruki encounter each other in the garden, it's also after closing time.

(GRACE enters the garden again, nearly running into HARUKI.)

HARUKI. You shouldn't be here.

GRACE. But here I am!

HARUKI. You should leave.

GRACE. What if I don't?

(*A moment.*)

Sorry. I don't mean to bother you. I'm just...

(*Tears well up in her, and she puts her hand
on her mouth, pressing the emotions back
and away.*)

HARUKI. Sudden little storm, out of nowhere?

GRACE. I'm not usually like this. I'm never like this. I
usually only cry in parking garages.

HARUKI. I would give you my handkerchief, but you still
haven't returned it from the last time.

GRACE. It's okay. I'll use my sleeve like a barbarian.

(*She uses her sleeve.*)

I'm okay!

HARUKI. Really?

GRACE. You're not supposed to ask that. You're supposed
to just go along with me when I say it, like everybody
else.

(*A moment.*)

How is the tea house coming along?

HARUKI. Great!

GRACE. Really?

(**HARUKI** *crumples up another drawing, and
throws it on the ground, and then stomps on
it.*)

(**GRACE** *laughs. Then she takes a little bamboo basket out of her bag. She takes a cloth napkin out of her bag, and lays it on the bench beside her.*)

HARUKI. What is this?

GRACE. My dinner. Pork bao.

(**GRACE** *opens the little bamboo basket.*)

HARUKI. Chinese food in a Japanese garden?

GRACE. I'm writing about China.

(*Beat.*)

Did you know that almost every culture makes some sort of little food wrapped in dough? Empanadas. Hand pies. Spring rolls. But bao are best.

HARUKI. Why?

GRACE. They're filled with <u>pork</u>.

(**GRACE** *looks up at* **HARUKI.**)

Would you like some?

(**GRACE** *holds out a pair of chopsticks.* **HARUKI** *takes them, then eats a bao.*)

(*It is good.*)

Have another. They're small.

HARUKI. I didn't realize I was hungry.

(**HARUKI** *takes another bao.*)

TOMMY Z. Between strange encounters with homeless girls and Japanese architects in the garden, Grace has one doctors appointment after another.

KAT. The third time Grace runs into Haruki in the garden, she has a problem she doesn't know how to solve.

> (**GRACE** *steps suddenly into* **HARUKI**'*s space, startling him.*)

GRACE. Do you drive? Know how to drive, I mean?

HARUKI. You are the strangest woman I have ever met.

GRACE. Sorry.

HARUKI. Yes. I know how to drive. I am better with automatic transmissions than stick shift transmissions, and with driving on the right side of the road than the left side.

GRACE. I need a favor.

> (*A moment.*)

I shouldn't ask you. But I feel like we've bonded a little bit through these little sessions where you try to throw me out of the garden.

> (*Beat.*)

Kat doesn't drive. My friend Kat, who... well, never mind that. They won't let me drive after... apparently I'm going to be kind of stoned afterwards. They give you some pretty strong anesthesia... and they want someone to stay during the procedure, just in case I... I don't know. I considered hiring an Uber driver, but I don't think the nurses would go for it. They're pretty sharp. Or the Uber driver. He'd probably bail, and then where would I be?

HARUKI. I have no idea what you are asking me.

GRACE. I should carry around a little piece of paper that has the whole thing written down on it, so I wouldn't have to tell anyone else. I really hate telling people. I should carry a flask full of some sort of really strong alcohol and a little piece of paper that has the whole thing written down on it, so I could...

(Beat.)

I have breast cancer.

> (**HARUKI** *doesn't move, but something inside him shifts.*)

It's a little bit... uh...

(Beat.)

So I'm getting everything checked. Everything I can think of. Skin today! Tomorrow they're going to put a camera up my... I can't even say it.

(Pause.)

Would you drive me to the doctor tomorrow, and stay in the waiting room while they check and see if I have cancer anywhere else, and then drive me home?

(Pause.)

I don't know why I'm asking you.

(Beat.)

I don't know who else to ask.

(A moment.)

I feel like it's everywhere. I could be teeming with it. The doctor said it's not very likely that it's... most likely it's contained, he doesn't think it's spread, they caught it early, he thinks, but what if I'm teeming with it?

HARUKI. Yes, I will drive you.

GRACE. *(Beat.)* Yes?

(A moment.)

TOMMY Z. The next morning, Haruki picks up Grace and her strange companion.

KAT. And then Kat and Haruki are in the hospital waiting room.

TOMMY Z. Waiting.

> *(Beat.)*

Waiting.

> *(Beat.)*

Waiting.

> (**HARUKI** *sits on the bench in the hospital waiting room, beside* **KAT**, *who is carrying* **GRACE**'s *purse awkwardly.*)

KAT. I don't think they believe we're her family.

HARUKI. Don't we look like America?

KAT. We didn't know the answers to any of the questions.

MALE NURSE. *(Voiced by* **TOMMY Z.**) Allergies?

HARUKI. I do not know.

MALE NURSE. Insurance number?

KAT. Maybe it's in her purse...

HARUKI. She gave this information already to the other nurse.

MALE NURSE. Oh-kay!

> *(The* **NURSE** *hands* **HARUKI** *a piece of paper with a number on it.*)

HARUKI. What is this?

MALE NURSE. Her number. Watch the board, and you can see when she's done. 407.

HARUKI. Four-zero-seven.

> *(The* **NURSE** *points at the board, and* **HARUKI** *and* **KAT** *look up at it.)*

KAT. How long?

MALE NURSE. We're a little backed up today.

> *(The* **NURSE** *goes.)*

> *(A long moment.)*

> *(Then, simultaneously:)*

| **HARUKI.** | **KAT.** |
| I hate hospitals. | I hate hospitals. |

> *(A moment.)*

HARUKI. You first.

KAT. Sometimes they lock you in.

> *(***HARUKI*** nods.)*

HARUKI. When you hurt yourself?

> *(***KAT*** pulls her sleeves down farther over her wrists, then nods.)*

KAT. How did you know that?

HARUKI. I look carefully. I see things.

KAT. Is that your superpower?

HARUKI. Super power? Like Gekko Kamen? Or... uh... Batman?

KAT. Tommy Z says everyone has a superpower.

> *(***HARUKI*** thinks about this a moment, amused at the notion. Without thinking about it, he begins to fold the little piece of paper with*

GRACE*'s number on it.* KAT *watches him,
curious.)*

HARUKI. "Tommy Z" sounds like a superhero name.

KAT. *(Agreeing.)* He saved me.

(TOMMY *looks over at* KAT, *surprised to find
himself in this part of the story.)*

(A moment.)

How about you? Why do you hate hospitals?

HARUKI. My wife died from cancer in hospital.

(Pause.)

Don't tell Grace.

KAT. I won't.

(Beat.)

I didn't know you had a wife.

HARUKI. Why wouldn't I have a wife?

KAT. You're very stern-looking.

HARUKI. I am not stern-looking.

(Beat.)

Maybe a little stern-looking.

(Beat.)

Are you how you look?

KAT. I don't know.

(Pause.)

How do I look?

HARUKI. Like a little fox during fox-hunting season.

(HARUKI hands KAT the tiny paper fox he has folded. KAT looks at it oddly.)

It was a long time ago.

KAT. Your wife dying?

(HARUKI nods.)

HARUKI. Ten years.

KAT. Ten years.

(Beat.)

What was her name?

HARUKI. Hiro.

(Beat.)

We were Hiro and Haruki.

(He remembers.)

(KAT nods.)

TOMMY Z. Ping!

(HARUKI and KAT look up at the board.)

A number lights up on the wall. 407.

HARUKI. Her number is there.

(And suddenly GRACE is there, launched out of the darkness, guided by the NURSE. HARUKI and KAT stand.)

GRACE. Hi!!

(GRACE's words don't stop as tidily as usual, and there's something rounder about her vowels. She has no idea how loud she's speaking, and very few inhibitions.)

The doctor gave me some "I don't care" medicine. That's what he called it. He had an accent. Maybe Bosnian. I did a brochure about Bosnia two years ago. It's hard to sell tourists on a place where there's been a mass genocide, but I did my best. They have wonderful sarma. That's a food.

KAT. You're really high.

GRACE. That's why they didn't want me to drive.

> (GRACE *touches* HARUKI's *face.*)

I don't have cancer in my bowels. They're as clean as a whistle. Maybe he's Armenian.

> (GRACE *lists to one side, and* HARUKI *catches her and sets her back on her feet as she continues to talk.*)

He was way nicer than you'd think somebody would be whose job it is to stick a camera up your ass. But he wouldn't give me more to take home with me.

> (HARUKI *and* KAT *look at each other, mystified.*)

KAT. More what?

GRACE. I don't care medicine. I told him I could use a shit load of that right now.

HARUKI. Would you like to go home?

GRACE. Okay.

TOMMY Z. Haruki and Kat take Grace home.

> (HARUKI *and* KAT *guide* GRACE *gently into her favorite chair.* KAT *pulls a blanket up over* GRACE. *And* GRACE *curls up under it and closes her eyes.*)

(**HARUKI** *looks around* **GRACE**'s *house,
curiously. Restlessly.*)

HARUKI. Very many books.

KAT. She likes books.

HARUKI. You are staying here, with Grace?

(**KAT** *nods.*)

KAT. She asked me to. If I wanted to.

HARUKI. And you did.

(**KAT** *nods.*)

Better than staying under a tree.

KAT. You knew I was there?

(**HARUKI** *gives* **KAT** *a sidelong glance.*)

You didn't say anything.

HARUKI. I'm very polite.

KAT. I was nervous about saying yes. I didn't know what
she wanted for it. But she seemed nice. Even before she
knew I was there, she seemed nice. And it had rained
seventeen days in a row. I was feeling really cold. Really
cold all the time.

(*Pause; with a bit of wonder.*)

She always has food in her refrigerator.

HARUKI. That is a very nice thing.

(*A moment.*)

KAT. You're building something.

HARUKI. Designing. Other people build.

KAT. Designing. How is the designing going?

HARUKI. Very bad.

KAT. What's very bad about it?

HARUKI. I am hired to design a tea house in the garden that is harumi... part of the nature? Not interrupting the nature. Build without building. Interrupt without interrupting. I do not know how to do it.

> *(Beat.)*

And now I am distracted.

> *(Pause.)*

I don't want to sit beside someone else's bedside while they die from cancer.

> *(**HARUK** looks over at **GRACE**, stricken, then rushes off.)*

GRACE. Do you think I'm going to die?

> *(**HARUKI** looks over at **GRACE**, stricken.)*

TOMMY Z. Haruki flees.

KAT. Grace and Kat watch him go.

> *(A moment.)*

TOMMY Z. Days go by. Grace cancels all of her shifts at the Japanese Garden as she prepares for her surgery. She tries not to think.

KAT. One day, she asks Kat...

GRACE. Would you like to go shopping with me?

KAT. What kind of shopping?

GRACE. I have to go to WalMart and buy a soft, white, cotton brassiere that hooks in the front. The nurse said... the nurse said I'll need one after the... because it will be hard to reach behind me for a while. She said they cost eight dollars and ninety seven cents at WalMart. I told her I don't shop at WalMart, on general principle...

(The lights shift.)

TOMMY Z. But suddenly, they are standing in the florescently-lit lingerie section at WalMart, in front of a rack of white cotton brassieres that hook in the front. A little sign with a smiley face on it says eight dollars and ninety seven cents.

*(**KAT** looks around nervously.)*

KAT. They'll think I'm shoplifting.

(Beat.)

They always think I'm shoplifting.

(Beat.)

Sometimes I am shoplifting.

GRACE. Have you shoplifted here?

KAT. I don't think so.

GRACE. Well, just stick close to me. I look innocuous, and I have three credit cards in my purse.

*(**GRACE** reaches out, resolutely, and takes a bra off the rack.)*

KAT. Are you going to try it on?

GRACE. No.

*(**GRACE** scowls at the brassiere.)*

You can't make anything good for eight dollars and ninety seven cents.

*(**GRACE** turns and looks at **KAT**.)*

Would you like some clothes? I'll buy you some clothes. If you'd like. I don't mean to... but it would be my pleasure. I have money. I don't really... spend it on anything. I just haven't... would you like some clothes? How about this. This would be a pretty color on you.

> (**GRACE** *takes a dress off a nearby rack. It's youthful and springy and simple and nice. Not too fancy. She holds it out to* **KAT**.)

> (**KAT**... *takes it.*)

KAT. In the dressing room, Kat takes off her layers of clothes, one by one, until she is in her underwear.

> (**KAT** *takes off her clothes, layer by layer, handing each item to* **GRACE**, *who she's pulled into the dressing room with her.*)

TOMMY Z. Grace can see tattoos on both of Kat's wrists, that transform the jagged scars from multiple suicide attempts.

> (*Beat.*)

When Kat slips the dress over her head, she looks lovely.

GRACE. You look lovely.

KAT. I should put it back.

GRACE. No!

> (*Beat.*)

No. Just give me the tag. I'll pay for it.

> (**GRACE** *pulls the tag off* **KAT**'s *dress.*)

> (**KAT** *grabs her clothes from* **GRACE** *and pulls them on over the dress, until she has all of her layers back in place.*)

TOMMY Z. Grace pays for everything, and then they go.

>   *(A moment.)*

Nine days later –

KAT. Nine days?

TOMMY Z. Nine days.

>   *(Beat.)*

Haruki is still trying to figure out how to design the tea house –

HARUKI. – and failing.

>   **(HARUKI** *balls up another drawing and throws it on the ground.)*

No one mentions, in architecture school, how much time you will spend figuring out how something won't work before you find the way it will.

KAT. He isn't just thinking about tea houses for those nine days.

TOMMY Z. <u>Nine days.</u>

KAT. He's also thinking about Grace.

HARUKI. Is she all right? Is she not all right? Is it any of my business? Why did she have to come into my garden, she is very distracting person. This is not what I came here for!

>   *(In Japanese, with the assumption that we will all continue to follow along: tr: I came here to work! I am trying to work!)*

Ole wa shigoto de kokoni kiteilun da! Shigoto ga shitain dayo! I am not a person who has time for...

KAT. Haruki finds that even in his head he has trouble saying the word "love."

(A moment.)

TOMMY Z. On the ninth day, Kat rushes into the garden.

KAT. Have you seen Grace?

HARUKI. No.

(Beat.)

What's wrong?

KAT. She hasn't come home. She should be home by now. It's late.

(Beat.)

Her surgery is tomorrow.

HARUKI. I know.

KAT. You have to help me find her. I don't know where she is! I don't know what she's doing! She could be in a... in a... bar! Or driving to the Grand Canyon! Or on a bridge somewhere, staring out into the dark, about to –

(The lights shift.)

*(And we see **GRACE**.)*

TOMMY Z. Grace <u>is</u> standing on a bridge! Somewhere. We can hear the traffic below, cars zooming by.

KAT. Grace opens her blouse and flashes the commuters below!

(There is a loud chorus of appreciative honks from the cars below.)

TOMMY Z. A uniformed policeman approaches.

*(The cop approaches **GRACE** warily.)*

COP. *(Voiced by **TOMMY Z.**)* Ma'am!

(Pause.)

Ma'am?

*(**GRACE** lets her blouse fall shut, and turns toward the **POLICEMAN**.)*

GRACE. Yes?

COP. What... uh... brings you up here this evening, ma'am?

GRACE. I'm flashing the cars down there.

COP. You need to stop.

GRACE. But they like it! Watch this.

*(**GRACE** turns and opens her blouse to the traffic again. Lots of honks! Including the long, low pull of a truck horn.)*

I love truck horns.

COP. *(Trying to establish some rapport.)*

Who doesn't love a truck horn?

(Beat.)

You're gonna need to button up, ma'am. And go home.

GRACE. I don't want to go home.

*(**GRACE** stares out into the darkness.)*

I don't usually stand on overpasses, flashing traffic.

COP. What made you decide to start today?

GRACE. I have breast cancer.

(Beat.)

I'm having surgery tomorrow.

COP. Oh, wow.

GRACE. Yeah.

COP. I'm sorry.

GRACE. Yeah.

COP. My aunt had breast cancer.

GRACE. What happened?

COP. She... uh... uh...

>   *(**GRACE** turns to the **COP**.)*

GRACE. Died?! She died?!

COP. Uh... yeah.

GRACE. Why did you just tell me that?!!

COP. I'm sorry!

GRACE. You should have lied!

COP. I can see that now!

>   *(**GRACE** turns toward traffic and flashes them again.)*

>   *(Horns honk loudly!)*

Ma'am!!

>   *(**GRACE** turns toward the **COP**, letting her blouse fall closed.)*

I really, really don't want to arrest you.

GRACE. Because I remind you of your dead aunt?

COP. No! No. No. Because...

>   *(**GRACE** buttons up her blouse.)*

GRACE. I'm usually very law-abiding.

COP. That's... uh... good.

GRACE. I couldn't go to a bar. I'm not supposed to drink right before the surgery. Which is a really bullshit rule, if you ask me, because I could really use a drink right now.

COP. So you decided to do this?

GRACE. "Decided" might be too strong a word. It was pretty spontaneous.

COP. *(Beat.)* Can I ...uh... do you need a ride somewhere? Or for me to call someone for you?

GRACE. Who would you call?

COP. Don't you have people?

GRACE. *(Beat.)* Difficult question.

> *(A moment.)*

TOMMY Z. Grace drives aimlessly through the darkness. And finds herself in the garden again.

> *(**KAT** and **HARUKI** notice her at the same time.)*

HARUKI.	**KAT.**
Grace!	Grace!

> *(**KAT** goes to **GRACE**.)*

KAT. Where have you been? I looked everywhere.

GRACE. I've been...

> *(**GRACE** glances at **HARUKI**, then back at **KAT**.)*

KAT. I got us a ride for tomorrow. Haruki is going to drive us.

> *(**HARUKI** looks at **KAT**, surprised.)*

*(To **HARUKI**.)* Right?

GRACE. It's too much to ask.

HARUKI. No, it isn't.

GRACE. *(To* **KAT.***)* We already have a ride for tomorrow. I
ordered us an Uber.

> *(Beat.)*

"Uber." What kind of stupid name is that?

KAT. You'll have to cancel it.

GRACE. I paid them already.

KAT. That's not how it works. You don't pay for it until –

HARUKI. <u>Grace.</u>

GRACE. She told me about your wife.

> *(***HARUKI** *looks at the ground.)*

> *(A moment.)*

Let's go home, Kat.

HARUKI. No.

> *(Beat.)*

Don't go.

> *(***GRACE** *pauses.)*

> *(***KAT** *looks between* **GRACE** *and* **HARUKI.***)*

> *(A moment.)*

I'm going to make you tea.

> *(Pause.)*

Can you have tea?

GRACE. That's about all I <u>can</u> have tonight.

HARUKI. Sit.

(Pause.)

Please.

> *(**GRACE** sits down on the bench, in the garden, and **KAT** sits on the ground beside her, and from somewhere, **HARUKI** conjures up a tray that holds a pot of steaming hot tea and three small cups. The tea set is clearly old, and beautifully crafted.)*

> *(**HARUKI** pours the tea, and hands cups to **GRACE** and **KAT**. All three of them drink.)*

GRACE. This tea set is beautiful.

> *(**GRACE** raises her cup to the light. A crack, which has been mended with gold, gleams.)*

There's a crack in the cup. Mended with gold.

HARUKI. Yes.

GRACE. I don't remember the word for that.

HARUKI. Kintsugi.

GRACE. *(Tasting the word.)* Kintsugi...

HARUKI. Belonged to my parents, this tea set. Wedding gift from their parents.

GRACE. You bring it with you when you travel?

HARUKI. I do.

GRACE. *(Remembering/quoting.)* "If man has no tea in him, he is incapable of understanding truth and beauty." Japanese proverb.

HARUKI. "There's a crack in everything. That's how the light gets in." Leonard Cohen.

> *(**GRACE** smiles.)*

(**HARUKI** *smiles back. And pours more tea.*)

(*They drink.*)

GRACE. It's hard to wait.

(*Pause.*)

Tick, tick, tock goes the click, click, clock. My father used to say.

(*Pause.*)

I can hear it.

TOMMY Z. We can hear it, too.

(*Beat.*)

Tick, tick, tock. Tick. Tick. Tock.

GRACE. Forboding.

HARUKI. (*Carefully.*) "Forboding?"

GRACE. It means... having a strong feeling that something terrible is going to happen.

HARUKI. You have the super power of Finding Perfect Words to Describe Things that Makes Us Feel Them in Our Hearts.

(**KAT** *looks at* **HARUKI.**)

(*Superpowers.*)

GRACE. What kind of ridiculous super power is that to have?

HARUKI. It is a very strong and amazing super power.

(**HARUKI** *looks at* **GRACE.**)

What time do we have to be there in the morning?

KAT. Seven thirty.

GRACE. Seven thirty.

HARUKI. Seven thirty.

> *(A moment.)*

KAT. Grace and Kat go home. And after Kat has gone to bed, and Grace is alone, Grace takes out her cell phone.

> *(In the privacy of her bedroom,* **GRACE** *stands in front of her mirror.)*

She stands in front of the mirror, looking at herself, the way she looks now, and never will again.

> *(Beat.)*

She takes three pictures of herself in the mirror.

TOMMY Z. Click. Click. Click.

> *(A moment.)*

KAT. The day of the surgery...

TOMMY Z. Haruki picks Grace and Kat up in the half-light, before dawn, so they can be at the hospital by seven-thirty.

> *(Beat.)*

Haruki and Kat are not sure what to do with themselves when the nurse takes Grace away from them.

KAT. But she's going to a place they can't follow.

> *(**GRACE** steps forward, and speaks to the audience.)*

GRACE. The day of the surgery was so strange. And long. Long and strange. The doctor comes in and says –

SURGEON. *(Voiced by* **TOMMY.***)* Which breast are we mutilating today?

GRACE. No... no, that's not what he said. But that's what I heard.

> *(Beat.)*

They keep double checking with me, over and over. "Why are you here?" "Why are you here?" It's good that they double check. It's really important that they double check. The horror stories you hear... "Oh, my God! They cut off the wrong leg! And I was here for an appendectomy!" But it's really hard to say it. Over and over again.

NURSE. *(Voiced by* **TOMMY.***)* Why are you here?

GRACE. Lumpectomy. I'm here for a...

NURSE. Which breast?

GRACE. Left breast.

NURSE. Which breast?

GRACE. Left breast.

NURSE. Why are you here?

GRACE. Breast cancer. Breast cancer. Breast cancer. Breast cancer. Breast cancer. I have breast cancer.

> *(A moment.)*

They take my blood pressure and wash my skin with something darker and more foul-smelling than bleach and write on my breast with a permanent black marker, and every minute is inching closer to the minute when they take out their knives.

> *(A moment.)*

The day lasts a million years and there is no part of it that isn't terrifying.

> *(Beat.)*

I don't want to be here. I don't want to be here. Would they notice if I slipped out the back in my stylish blue hospital gown, down Oak Street, past the grocery store, and just kept going?

> *(Beat.)*

I stay.

> *(Beat.)*

I let them.

> *(Beat.)*

"Save" me?

> *(A moment.)*

> *(And then* **GRACE** *is being discharged from the hospital. She is dizzy and in pain and curls around herself protectively and can't stand by herself and doesn't want to be touched.)*

> *(**HARUKI** and **KAT** get **GRACE** home, and she settles carefully into her chair.)*

KAT. Eleven hours later, when Haruki and Kat finally get Grace home, she lies back in her big chair, very still. Not moving.

> *(**GRACE** lies in her chair.)*

> *(Very still.)*

> *(Not moving.)*

Now she waits?

TOMMY Z. Now she waits. For the pathology report. Which will explain how bad the cancer is, and how much it's spread, and what happens next.

KAT. Pathology.

TOMMY Z. Ten days.

KAT. Ten days.

> (**GRACE** *opens her eyes, but doesn't move from her cocoon of blankets.*)

GRACE. What did they find? Has it spread? Is it in my lymph nodes now? Did they get it all? Do they have to take more? Do they have to take everything?

> (*Pause.*)

I don't want them to take everything.

> (*A moment.*)

TOMMY Z. It takes Grace days to gather up the courage to take off the bandage and look at herself.

> (**GRACE** *opens up the top button of her shirt.*)
>
> (*She looks.*)
>
> (*Then she turns away from everything and everyone, and curls into herself.*)

KAT. Kat doesn't know what to do.

> (*Beat.*)

She thinks about running away. She thinks hard about that. She thinks about taking the forty dollars Grace has hidden in her underwear drawer and the three hundred dollars Grace has hidden in her battered copy of Moby Dick, and running back to the willow tree or some other tree or just away.

> (*Beat.*)

But she doesn't do any of these things.

(**KAT** *steps toward* **GRACE**.)

Would you like me to pull back the curtains?

GRACE. No.

KAT. It's really dark in here.

(**GRACE** *doesn't answer.*)

Would you like me to turn on the light?

GRACE. No.

(**KAT** *looks at* **GRACE**. *She takes a deep breath and gathers her courage. Then she goes and sits beside* **GRACE**.)

(*A moment.*)

KAT. I was sad for a long time, too.

(*A moment.*)

For a long time, I wanted someone to come and rescue me. But no one did.

(*Beat.*)

I never told you how I got my tattoos. On my wrists. Tommy Z gave them to me. His name is Tommy Z. Just the letter.

(*Beat.*)

I met him in the emergency room waiting room.

(*Beat.*)

The emergency room waiting room is kind of a strange place. Especially in the middle of the night.

(**KAT** *turns... and steps into her own memory.*)

TOMMY Z. Tommy Z is sitting there on the bench, waiting, waiting, waiting. How you do.

> (**TOMMY** *is exhausted and angry and he looks like the kind of person you should steer clear of, but* **KAT** *steps toward him anyway.*)

KAT. I'm sorry... can I ...? There aren't any other chairs.

TOMMY Z. Sit down. It's okay.

KAT. Crowded in here tonight.

TOMMY Z. There was a gang thing earlier. I'd keep clear of the Nazi wannabes over in the corner if I was you. They're still itching to start something with somebody.

> (**KAT** *looks over the Nazi wannabes nervously.*)

You want some coffee, kid? I got quarters.

KAT. I'm okay.

TOMMY Z. You look a little pale.

> (**KAT** *smiles a little.*)

KAT. What are you here for?

TOMMY Z. Overdose. My dumb ass brother. I fucking hate heroin.

> (*Pause.*)

You?

KAT. Kat slides her arms out of her sleeves. Her wrists drip blood all over the floor.

> (*Beat; to* **TOMMY**.)

It won't stop.

TOMMY Z. Oh, God.

(**TOMMY** *pulls a rag out of his pocket and winds it around* **KAT**'s *wrists. He holds her wrists tightly, trying to stop the bleeding.*)

(*Shouting over his shoulder.*)

We could use some help over here!!

(**KAT** *looks at her wrists, held tight in* **TOMMY** **Z**'s *hands. Then she looks up at him.*)

KAT. Is this going to be a sad story?

TOMMY Z. No! No.

KAT. Okay.

(**KAT**'s *eyes fall shut, and she lists a bit.*)

TOMMY Z. Stay with me!

(*Through the following,* **TOMMY** *works hard to keep* **KAT** *with him, and conscious, and distracted from what's happening to her.*)

KAT. He stayed with me while they sewed me up.

TOMMY Z. You with me?

KAT. Yes.

(*Beat.*)

They tried to kick him out, but he said I was his cousin.

TOMMY Z. Tommy Z.

KAT. Tommy Z ...?

(**KAT** *looks down at her wrists.*)

They use a curved needle and invisible thread.

(**KAT** *shudders.*)

TOMMY Z. Look here, okay?

KAT. Okay.

>*(Beat.)*

Is that your real name?

TOMMY Z. It's what people call me.

>*(Beat.)*

What's your name, kid?

KAT. Kat. Is what people call me.

>*(**KAT** slumps a little, and **TOMMY** tries to keep her with him.)*

TOMMY Z. No! Look here, okay? Look at me, Kat.

KAT. Will you talk to me?

TOMMY Z. I don't know what to say. What am I supposed to say?

KAT. Anything.

TOMMY Z. People tell <u>me</u> things. When I'm working on them.

>*(Beat.)*

I got a shop down on Highwater. A tattoo shop.

KAT. Tattoo shop...

TOMMY Z. Yeah.

>*(Beat.)*

All kinds of people come in. All kinds. And every one of them has a story.

>*(Beat.)*

This one guy, he was a fireman.

KAT. A fireman.

TOMMY Z. One of those guys who goes out when whole forests are on fire. He got burned really bad. His whole back was... He had trouble breathing, because his lungs were messed up, so I remember the sound of his breathing while I worked on him.

> *(Beat.)*

He told me to draw anything, he just needed it to be something different than what was there. So I drew a forest. Fir trees. Pine trees. Oak trees. Birch trees.

KAT. Birds?

> **(TOMMY** *nods.)*

TOMMY Z. A fox. A little stream, running through it.

KAT. A little stream...

TOMMY Z. It took three weeks to do. And he'd been silent the whole time, except for the sound of his breathing. But about halfway through, he started talking. Telling me what happened on that day when the fire got him.

> *(Beat.)*

Sometimes I think the whole job is trying to put in windows where there used to be walls, so the light can get in.

KAT. There's a lot of darkness.

TOMMY Z. *(Beat.)* Yeah.

> **(KAT** *looks into* **TOMMY**'s *eyes, with a sudden and surprising clarity.)*

KAT. You're a window-put-er.

TOMMY Z. Window-put-er.

> *(Smiling a little.)*

I guess everybody has their own weird-ass superpower.

(A moment.)

(Then **TOMMY** *takes the rag from* **KAT**'s *wrists.)*

Do you want me to...

(A moment.)

KAT. And then he offered to tattoo my wrists. If I wanted. As a... I don't know. As a something. And I said yes.

(A moment.)

I wanted the light to get in.

*(***KAT*** *turns back to* **GRACE**.*)*

Do you want the light to get in?

*(***GRACE*** *doesn't move. But she's heard what* **KAT** *is trying to tell her.)*

TOMMY Z. Haruki comes to the house, to check on Grace.

*(***GRACE*** *is still sitting alone in her chair.)*

*(***HARUKI*** *watches her for a moment.)*

HARUKI. You need to get up.

GRACE. *(Pause; flatly.)* Do I?

HARUKI. The doctor said you should walk. You should take walks.

TOMMY Z. Grace doesn't get up.

KAT. She takes a bag of frozen peas out from under her shirt.

GRACE. Will you put this back in the freezer for me and get me a fresh bag?

(**HARUKI** *takes the bag of peas and looks at it oddly.*)

HARUKI. Would you like to stick with peas, or change to another vegetable?

GRACE. Peas, please. Sorry. Thank you. Sorry.

HARUKI. Don't be sorry. I've never been given the peas off a woman's breast before.

GRACE. What's left of it.

(*A moment.*)

Sorry.

HARUKI. For being sad that something was taken from you?

GRACE. Yes.

(*Beat.*)

I'm not doing a very good job right now at not being sad.

HARUKI. Maybe that's not your job.

(*Beat.*)

Maybe your job right now is being sad.

(**GRACE** *doesn't move.*)

We could go to the garden.

(**GRACE** *turns her head and looks at* **HARUKI.**)

(*When he extends his hand to her, she takes it, and rises shakily from her chair.*)

(*The lights shift.*)

KAT. The light changes into dappled golden sunlight. The air smells like moss and Japanese lilac.

(Beat.)

The sound of wind ruffling leaves. The sound of a bird calling another bird.

*(**GRACE** smiles. It is so peaceful here.)*

HARUKI. Would you like to sit down?

GRACE. We just got here.

(But she does. And they do. They sit on the bench for a moment, still holding hands.)

Do Japanese people believe in heaven?

HARUKI. It depends on the Japanese person.

GRACE. Do you believe in heaven?

HARUKI. I don't know.

GRACE. Have you thought about it?

HARUKI. Yes.

GRACE. *(Beat.)* When your wife died?

HARUKI. Yes.

(A moment.)

GRACE. Was she very beautiful?

HARUKI. She was very beautiful to me.

(Pause.)

She's been gone a long time now.

GRACE. You still miss her.

HARUKI. Yes.

(A moment.)

How do you come to be so alone?

GRACE. I didn't mean to.

(*Pause.*)

I was married once.

HARUKI. Yes?

GRACE. For about five minutes. A long time ago. Neither one of us had any idea what we were doing.

(*Beat.*)

My ex-husband and his wife have three kids. And a house with a yard and a dog. And I do NOT want him back. But I've sometimes felt like that's the alternative universe life that's supposed to belong to me.

(*Pause.*)

How about you?

HARUKI. Me?

GRACE. Ten years since your wife died.

HARUKI. It is better to be alone than to allow your heart to be ripped out of your chest again.

(*Pause.*)

This is what I have thought for a long time.

GRACE. Is that what you still think?

HARUKI. (*Pause.*) It is hard to be without when you know what it's like to be with.

(**HARUKI** *and* **GRACE** *continue to sit where they are, on the bench, holding hands, but the light shifts around them, to something more ominous and florescent.*)

TOMMY Z. And then the ten days are up. And Grace and Haruki are in an examining room at the hospital. And the doctor is looking at the pathology report.

SURGEON. *(Voiced by* **TOMMY Z.***)* I'm sorry.

> *(***GRACE** *pulls her hand out of* **HARUKI**'s *hand, and crosses her arms across her chest protectively.)*

GRACE. More surgery.

SURGEON. I know that's not what you wanted to hear.

GRACE. Do you... do you have to do a...

SURGEON. Re-excision. Is what we call it. To get a safe margin around the site. We'll just take out a little more tissue.

> *(To* **HARUKI.***)*

We call it a lumpectomy, but that doesn't always mean there's an actual, discrete lump that we can just take out. In...

> *(The doctor's eyes dip toward* **GRACE**'s *chart to check her name.)*

... Grace's case, it was more of a...

> *(The surgeon makes an odd, flickering gesture with his fingers.)*

GRACE. *(Flatly.)* Constellation.

SURGEON. Yes! Exactly. Great word. More of a constellation of cancer cells across the top of the breast.

GRACE. I don't want a mastectomy.

> *(***HARUKI** *looks at the floor.)*

SURGEON. Nothing's sure. But I think I can get it with a re-excision.

(Pause.)

How does May 3rd look for you?

GRACE. You can't do it this week?

SURGEON. We have to let you heal a little more.

GRACE. Before you cut me open again.

SURGEON. I really think I can get it this time.

(The light shifts.)

*(**GRACE** goes back to her chair, and curls up in it.)*

*(**HARUKI** watches her.)*

(A moment.)

HARUKI. Are you hurting?

GRACE. No.

(Pause.)

Not much.

HARUKI. Do you need a pain pill?

GRACE. It's not that.

(Pause.)

Do you ever find yourself grieving for the selves you'll never be?

HARUKI. What do you mean?

GRACE. I'm forty six years old. You're even older than that. Don't give me that look. You are.

(Beat.)

It's very difficult to realize, to come to terms with the fact, that there's all sorts of things I imagined I'd be in my life that I'm not actually going to.

HARUKI. Like what?

GRACE. Helicopter nurse!

HARUKI. Someone who nurses helicopters back to good working?

GRACE. No, silly. Someone who rides around in a helicopter, saving people.

HARUKI. I don't know if that's really a job.

GRACE. It's definitely a job!

HARUKI. Okay.

GRACE. Painter of medieval manuscripts!

(**HARUKI** *gives* **GRACE** *an odd look.*)

What?!

HARUKI. I've never known anyone who spoke in as many exclamation points as you do.

GRACE. I'm a very emphatic person.

HARUKI. I don't think they have painters of medieval manuscripts anymore.

GRACE. I bet the Metropolitan Museum of Art employs at least three.

HARUKI. Maybe.

GRACE. Mother.

(*Pause.*)

Did you and your wife want to have children?

(*Pause.*)

You don't have to answer that. I'm always asking questions that are too personal, which is probably why I can count the number of friends I have on –

HARUKI. Yes.

> *(There is a long moment, as they think about the parents they will never be.)*

Baseball player.

GRACE. Baseball player?

> *(HARUKI nods.)*

HARUKI. Astronaut.

GRACE. I can totally see that. Giant helmet and everything.

> *(A moment.)*

I thought there would be more having before there was losing.

> *(HARUKI nods. Him, too.)*

> *(They are very close to each other.)*

I don't know how you got here. How did you get here?

HARUKI. I flew in an airplane.

> *(GRACE laughs.)*

First class.

GRACE. I've been alone for a million years.

HARUKI. Me, too.

> *(Beat.)*

I find that I would like to kiss you.

GRACE. This is a terrible time to fall in love with someone!!

HARUKI. I'm not in love with you!!

> (**HARUKI** *gets clumsily to his feet, but then isn't sure what to do with himself.*)

> (*A moment.*)

GRACE. You should go.

TOMMY Z. Haruki flees.

> (**GRACE** *watches him go.*)

GRACE. When the storm rages || what will become of my boat? || I am untethered.

KAT. Haiku.

> (*A moment.*)

Grace's second surgery happens. She and Kat really do take an Uber to get there this time, because Haruki still hasn't come back.

GRACE. It's hard to be without when you know what it's like to be with.

> (**KAT** *nods.*)

KAT. And then it's time for radiation.

GRACE. I took an Uber by myself to get there.

KAT. You didn't have to.

GRACE. Yes, I did.

> (*A moment.*)

KAT. What was today?

GRACE. Simulation. They simulated me. In a simulator.

KAT. I don't know what that means.

GRACE. They put you in this giant machine, and make a map of the area they're going to radiate.

> *(The lights shift. And then* **GRACE** *steps into a small pool of bright, white light. There is an ominous mechanical hum as the machine starts up.)*

You have to put your arms up above your head.

> *(She puts her arms above her head.)*

And they put all these little stickers on you, and draw on your skin, and tattoo little dots on you, so they'll be able to laser position the machine exactly right every time.

> *(Beat.)*

And then you lie there, really, really still, while they close the big bank door between them, and you and the radiation, and then the machine goes around and around and around.

> *(The low, ominous hum of the simulator machine goes around and around and around.)*

> *(The light shifts.)*

> *(***HARUKI*** hands* **KAT** *a small paper crane that he has been folding.)*

> *(***KAT*** gives the crane to* **GRACE***.)*

TOMMY Z. On a Friday, at the end of Grace's first week of radiation therapy, she goes to the Japanese Garden.

> *(***GRACE*** steps into the garden, carrying a little brown paper lunch sack. She sees* **HARUKI***.)*

KAT. Haruki is there, sketching out ideas for his tea room, then crumpling them up and tossing them aside. There are lots of crumpled papers littered around him.

GRACE. Hello.

HARUKI. Hello.

> *(A long moment.)*

End of your first week of radiation therapy, yes?

> *(**GRACE** nods.)*

Kat told me.

> *(A moment.)*

GRACE. I got your note.

> *(**GRACE** holds out the paper crane.)*

No words on it.

HARUKI. Then how did you know it was from me?

> *(**GRACE** smiles.)*

How are you doing?

GRACE. The chirpy little med tech with too much make-up and feathered blond hair keeps asking me that.

KAT. Suddenly, the chirpy little blond med tech is there, in her mulberry scrubs, saying –

MED TECH. *(Voiced by **KAT**.)* How are YOU today?

GRACE. *(To **HARUKI**.)* And I know what she wants me to say.

MED TECH. How are YOU today?

GRACE. *(To the **MED TECH**.)* All right.

MED TECH. Let's get you up here on the table, okay?

GRACE. I'm not all right, I'm just saying that because she's not really asking-asking, she's polite-asking, and she has another person coming in fifteen minutes.

MED TECH. How ARE you today?

GRACE. She's disappointed in my answer. I can feel the disappointment rising off her in waves.

MED TECH. Would you like a warm blanket for your arms?

GRACE. She doesn't want me to be polite-lying-all-right as I –

MED TECH. Take a breath and hold it –

GRACE. – so they won't radiate too much of my heart and lungs.

MED TECH. Take a breath and hold it. That's it!

GRACE. I know what she wants.

MED TECH. How ARE YOU today?

GRACE. *(Suddenly matching the* **MED TECH***'s cheerfulness, and raising her one each time.)* Great!

MED TECH. *(Smiling! liking this so much better!)* How are you today?

GRACE. Awesome, Melanie! How are YOU?

MED TECH. *(Bigger and louder.)* How are you today?

GRACE. Fan-fucking-tastic!!

MED TECH. *(Bigger and louder.)* How are you today?!

GRACE. Ready to fight cancer and WIN!!!

MED TECH. *(Bigger and louder.)* That's what I like to hear!!!

        *(***GRACE** *turns to* **HARUKI***.)*

GRACE. But that's not how I feel.

HARUKI. How do you feel really?

GRACE. I don't want to talk about that.

>   *(Beat.)*

Want to have lunch with me? I brought cucumber sandwiches.

>   *(**GRACE** holds out the paper sack lunch.)*

HARUKI. Are you writing about England now?

GRACE. You are getting to know me way too well.

>   *(**HARUKI** takes the sack from **GRACE**.)*

What's wrong with all the crumpled papers?

HARUKI. They aren't better than what's here already.

GRACE. A bench under a tree?

>   *(**HARUKI** nods.)*

HARUKI. It's hard to beat a bench under a tree.

>   *(A moment.)*

I did not know if you would come back.

GRACE. I didn't know if I'd come back either.

>   *(A moment.)*

HARUKI. I can't stop thinking about you.

>   *(Beat.)*

I've tried.

>   *(**GRACE** laughs.)*

>   *(**HARUKI** puts his hand on his heart, because it is cracking open at the sound of **GRACE**'s laugh, then puts it down again.)*

Grace?

GRACE. Yes?

HARUKI. I have a house in Jiyugaoka, which I design and build. Three rooms that curve down along a hillside around a four hundred year old sakura tree. A small stream matches the curve of the house, and ends in a waterfall beside the deck, and a small pool with koi fishes.

GRACE. It sounds beautiful.

HARUKI. I am a very good architect.

> *(A moment.)*

It is very empty.

> *(**GRACE** nods.)*

Come with me.

GRACE. *(Beat.)* What are you talking about?

> *(**HARUKI** reaches out and takes **GRACE**'s hand, startling her. Then... he kisses her.)*
>
> *(She melts into the kiss for a moment, but then pulls away.)*

What are you doing?

HARUKI. Asking. I'm asking you to come with me. Back to Japan. Home with me. Be with me.

> *(**GRACE** moves away from **HARUKI**.)*

GRACE. Why are you asking me that? I feel really ugly right now! And lopsided.

HARUKI. When I tilt my head like this, you look just right.

GRACE. I'm wearing clothes.

> *(Beat.)*

I don't look just right when I'm not wearing clothes.

HARUKI. I can't see anything without my contacts.

> *(Beat.)*

I could take out my contacts.

GRACE. You have hands.

HARUKI. Do you want me to cut off my hands?

> *(HARUKI holds out his hands, and GRACE takes them, and shakes her head.)*

GRACE. No!

> *(A moment.)*

I <u>can't</u>.

KAT. Grace flees.

> *(GRACE hurries away from HARUKI, but then stops abruptly, and finds herself alone at the center of the stage.)*

TOMMY Z. The radiation treatments take forever and are done so suddenly.

GRACE. Now what do I do?

> *(GRACE looks down at herself, then up at all the doctors, all the nurses, all the med techs, all the everybody.)*

You're just going to leave me like this?

> *(A moment.)*

Am I safe now?

> *(A moment.)*

Is anybody there?

KAT. I'm here.

>   (**GRACE** *turns and looks at* **KAT**.)

Did you have a bad dream?

GRACE. No.

>   (**GRACE** *goes over and sits in her chair.* **KAT**
>   *tucks in beside her, and pulls the blanket over*
>   *their legs.*)

Haruki asked me to go to Japan with him.

KAT. He did?

>   (**GRACE** *nods.*)

What did you say?

GRACE. I couldn't. I can't.

>   (*Beat.*)

It's ridiculous. It's crazy.

>   (*A moment.*)

I want to.

>   (*Beat.*)

But...

>   (*Slowly and carefully,* **GRACE** *places her*
>   *fingers on* **KAT**'s *wrists.*)

>   (**KAT**... *lets her.*)

>   (**GRACE** *gently draws* **KAT**'s *sleeves up, so she*
>   *can see the tattooed scars on them.*)

They're beautiful. Your tattoos.

>   (*A moment.*)

Did it help?

KAT. Yes.

(A moment.)

GRACE. Do you think he'd help me?

KAT. Get a tattoo?

GRACE. Yes.

(Beat.)

I can't look at myself.

*(**KAT** pulls away from **GRACE**.)*

KAT. Tattoos aren't about beautifulness.

*(**KAT** looks over at **TOMMY**, remembering.)*

TOMMY Z. Some of them are beautiful, sure. Roses and dragons and sailing ships. But that's not the point. If it was just about that, you'd put it on your wall, not on your skin.

(Beat.)

You might not have words for what you want, or what you need. That's okay. I hear what you don't say.

(Beat.)

A tattoo is something you are choosing to wear forever. That's important. That word. Choosing.

(Beat.)

TOMMY Z & KAT. A tattoo is something you get to choose. Your story, written on your skin.

*(**KAT** turns back to **GRACE**.)*

GRACE. I understand.

(Beat.)

I want to own my own story again.

(Beat.)

Will you give me his number?

KAT. I have to check. To see if it's okay.

> (**KAT** *turns toward* **TOMMY**'s *tattoo shop. He is sitting there alone, in the dark, drinking.*)

The lights are out and the door is locked and the 'closed' sign is up when Kat appears on Tommy Z's doorstep. She pounds on his door until he opens it.

> (**TOMMY** *opens the door, but stands in the doorway, blocking it.*)

TOMMY Z. I'm closed, kid.

KAT. I need to talk to you.

TOMMY Z. Closed. <u>Closed</u>.

KAT. This is important.

> (**KAT** *slides under* **TOMMY**'s *arm and into the shop.*)

TOMMY Z. I am no longer in the tattooing business.

KAT. What are you talking about?

TOMMY Z. Get out of here. Okay?

KAT. No! My friend Grace needs your help. She's sad.

TOMMY Z. Everybody's sad.

KAT. She's stuck.

TOMMY Z. That's not my problem.

KAT. I told her about you.

TOMMY Z. What part of "I don't do that anymore" do you not understand?

KAT. It's wrong to not help if you know how to help.

TOMMY Z. I don't know how to help people.

KAT. Of course you do! You helped me. You helped that fireman. You helped your brother.

> (**TOMMY** *turns away from* **KAT**. *Moves away from her.*)

What's wrong?

TOMMY Z. I didn't.

KAT. *(Beat.)* What?

TOMMY Z. I didn't.

> *(Beat.)*

Help my brother.

> *(Beat.)*

He's dead.

KAT. What?

> *(A moment.)*

Oh...

TOMMY Z. Yeah.

> *(Beat.)*

So I'm closed now.

KAT. For how long?

> (**TOMMY** *doesn't answer.*)

This is your superpower.

TOMMY Z. This is not a comic book! Or a fairy tale! This is real life!

> *(Beat.)*

And what I do... what I did... it's not a superpower. It's not a... it's not free.

KAT. She has money. She can pay you.

TOMMY Z. That's not what I meant.

> *(A moment.)*

KAT. Kat leaves the tattoo shop. She doesn't know what to do...

> *(Beat.)*

So she goes to the garden.

> *(**KAT** goes to the garden, where **HARUKI** is sitting on the bench, folding a piece of paper.)*

Hi.

HARUKI. Hello.

> *(**KAT** moves closer to **HARUKI**, and watches him for a moment.)*

KAT. What are you making?

HARUKI. Not a tea house.

> *(**KAT** sits beside **HARUKI**, watching his hands as he folds the paper.)*

> *(**HARUKI** sees **KAT** watching him. He hands the paper to her.)*

> *(**KAT** takes it.)*

*(Through the following, HARUKI shows KAT,
step by step, how to fold an origami boat.)*

It is not so simple. To make something that is... more.
That is right. That is harumi. Kokoro-ippei. I don't
know how to say. I am famous architect. Very famous!
I know how to design a tea house. Wall, wall, wall, wall,
roof, done. But to make it...

(Gesturing at the heavens.)

This is not landscaping. This is not putting a shed to
hide the view of your neighbor's garbage bins.

*(HARUKI looks over at KAT's folding, and
corrects her.)*

(A little chiding sound.) Ch, ch, ch. Like this.

(KAT nods.)

It is a terrible darkness, when the person of your heart
is torn away from you.

(KAT nods.)

I have not been able to work like I worked before.
Broken pieces inside my chest. For a very long time.

(Beat.)

So no tea house.

(Beat.)

And then... a strange person comes into my garden and
asks me the most ridiculous question. I surprise myself
by saying yes. Because everything has been "no" for so
long.

*(KAT nods, and HARUKI helps her finish the
last folds on the boat. He hands her a pencil.)*

Write your message on the boat, and it will carry it into the receiver's heart.

(**KAT** *looks toward* **TOMMY**, *then writes her message on the boat.*)

Grace has gone. I do not know if she will return. But... there is a crack in everything now. Everything inside me. And... I find that I can hear what the earth whispers to me once again. And...

(**KAT** *holds out her boat.*)

(*Surprised, as the answer comes to him.*) Now I know how to do it.

TOMMY Z. Haruki didn't really tell Kat all that. What he really said was...

HARUKI. This is how you build a boat.

(**KAT** *goes to* **GRACE**'*s house and gives the boat to her.*)

(*A moment.*)

(*Then* **GRACE** *goes to the tattoo parlor.*)

GRACE. Are you Tommy Z?

(**TOMMY** *looks at* **GRACE** *blankly.*)

Kat gave me your address.

TOMMY Z. I'm closed.

GRACE. I can come back tomorrow.

TOMMY Z. I'm closed for good, lady. Finito. I might burn the whole place down, I don't know, I haven't decided yet.

GRACE. Kat said you could help me.

TOMMY Z. I told Kat I don't do that anymore.

GRACE. I need your help.

> *(Beat.)*

On the outside, when I'm wearing clothes, I look just the same as I did before. I didn't even lose my hair.

> *(Beat.)*

But I'm not the same.

> **(GRACE** *opens her blouse and lets* **TOMMY** *see.)*

> **(TOMMY** *looks at her. At the jagged, damaged place where the scar is.)*

> **(GRACE** *closes her blouse with one clenched fist.)*

Sorry.

TOMMY Z. Why are you sorry?

GRACE. I don't know.

> *(A moment.)*

I'm ugly. I'm... ugly. I feel so –

TOMMY Z. I can't do what you're asking me to do!

GRACE. Why not?

> *(A moment.)*

TOMMY Z. Every time my brother got low, he'd get high.

> **(GRACE** *listens.)*

Sometimes I could... if I could find him, or if he called me before he found his dealer, or if he was broke and came to me for cash, sometimes I could keep him from... I could keep him from... I could keep him from shooting up by tattooing him. Something about... the sound of the machine and the feel of the needle on his skin. And I'd talk to him while I... And I'd go really slow, as slow as I could, sometimes all night, I'd... so maybe he wouldn't hit me and take the cash in the register and go fucking kill himself, but you can't save people.

(*Pause.*)

And that's what you're here asking me, is if I'll save you, and I can't fucking bear it.

GRACE. I'm not asking you to save me. I'm just...

(*Beat.*)

I'm tired of darkness.

(*Beat.*)

I want to let the light in.

(**TOMMY** *shakes his head. He can't do this.*)

(*He can't.*)

TOMMY Z. I can't.

(**GRACE** *takes a breath, then lets it out. She doesn't know what to do now. Go?*)

GRACE. Kat asked me to give this to you.

(**GRACE** *drops the tiny folded paper boat into* **TOMMY**'*s hands, then goes.*)

(**TOMMY** *reads the note, then bows his head, then looks out at the audience.*)

TOMMY Z. In tiny, careful letters, Kat had written...

KAT. There's a lot of darkness.

(**TOMMY** *looks over at* **KAT.** *Then goes after* **GRACE.**)

TOMMY Z. Wait.

> (**GRACE** *turns.*)

Are you done? With all the treatments and surgeries? Fixed?

GRACE. I don't know if I ever get to be sure of that.

TOMMY Z. What happens now?

GRACE. They release me back into the wild, like a fish. Like a little rainbow trout, back in the water and able to breathe again, bloody mouth and a story to tell all the other little fishes back home about its near-death experience.

> (*A moment.*)

TOMMY Z. It hurts. To do this.

GRACE. (*Beat.*) It looks like it hurts to not do it, too.

> (*Pause.*)

I'm sorry about your brother.

> (**TOMMY** *nods.*)

> (**GRACE** *turns and moves away.*)

TOMMY Z. Okay.

> (**GRACE** *turns back to* **TOMMY.**)

GRACE. Okay?

> (**TOMMY** *nods.*)

TOMMY Z. Okay.

> (**TOMMY** *gestures for* **GRACE** *to go back into his tattoo shop, and sit down.*)

(He wheels himself over to her, until they are knee to knee.)

*(**GRACE** opens her blouse. She holds it away from her breast, and **TOMMY** puts his hand over her hand.)*

*(**GRACE** and **TOMMY** look at each other.)*

GRACE. What are you going to draw?

TOMMY Z. Tommy tattoos words on Grace's breast, along the edge of her scars. Like a promise. Like a vow.

GRACE. Like a covenant.

TOMMY Z. This is not the end. This is the beginning.

*(**GRACE** looks at her new tattoo, then grabs hold of **TOMMY**'s hands, not sure how to thank him.)*

GRACE. I never, ever imagined I would get a tattoo.

TOMMY Z. Special circumstances.

*(**GRACE** nods. Then steps out of the tattoo parlor. Back toward the world.)*

GRACE. *(To the audience.)* I can look at myself now.

(The lights shift.)

KAT. Grace gathers up all of her courage, and goes back to the garden.

*(**HARUKI** is finished with his tea house.)*

(Which is just the same bench that was there before, in a space defined by beams but without walls, open to the garden, cradled by the trees, dappled in golden sunlight.)

(It's just right.)

GRACE. You finished the tea house!

HARUKI. Yes.

> (**GRACE** *looks at the tea house for a long moment, taking it in.* **KAT** *and* **TOMMY** *do, too.)*

GRACE. It's beautiful.

HARUKI. Yes.

GRACE. *(Beat.)* So you're going?

HARUKI. *(Pause.)* I find that what I have built here... I do not want to leave.

> *(A moment.)*

For three months, I have been sitting in this garden, with everything I ever thought I knew about the world called into question.

> *(A moment.)*

I will tell you a story that goes far away but comes back to this.

GRACE. Okay.

HARUKI. Whenever I go to Tokyo, Akiko Yamamoto makes dinner for me at her home. My wife's most dear friend. Friend to both of us through everything.

> *(Beat.)*

Lawyer. She is a lawyer who also goes out into small boats to fight for the whales? So crazy. But also fierce. Everyone has always been a little bit afraid of Akiko.

> *(Pause.)*

So we are having a drink after dinner and talking about the old days together. And then our new projects that we are working on. And she says...

AKIKO. *(Voiced by* **KAT.***)* I wish you would make something with your heart in it again.

HARUKI. *(Tr: Japanese bush warbler.)* And all my feathers ruffle, like a little uguisu bird. And I say, "Everything I design has my heart in it!" And she says...

AKIKO. Everything you have designed since Hiro died is cold. Beautiful. Impressive. Smart. But cold.

> *(A moment.)*

Hiro would be sad if the last thing you ever made with your heart in it was the house she never got to live in.

> *(A moment.)*

HARUKI. I had made four big projects in a row. Hotel in Dubai. Art museum in Copenhagen. Conference center in Bogota. Music hall in Lagos. And when I thought back on them, I thought... maybe Akiko the Merciless is not wrong.

> *(Beat.)*

So! When I receive a most humble request to design this humble Japanese tea house in this humble Japanese Garden for a most humble amount of money, I say yes. I will come in three days.

> *(Pause.)*

And now here I sit.

GRACE. How did you finally figure it out? After all the crumpled papers?

HARUKI. You have given me back my heart.

> (**GRACE** *smiles at* **HARUKI**, *unsure of herself. Hoping.)*

GRACE. Do you still want me to come with you?

HARUKI. *(Beat.)* Yes.

> *(Beat.)*

<u>Yes.</u>

GRACE. YES.

> (**GRACE** *and* **HARUKI** *kiss.*)

HARUKI. What made you change your mind?

GRACE. Kintsugi.

> *(Beat.)*

I'm not perfect.

HARUKI. I'm not perfect either.

> *(Beat.)*

We can be not perfect together.

GRACE. Okay.

HARUKI. Okay.

> *(They kiss again.)*

> *(Then* **GRACE** *turns to the audience.)*

GRACE. You'll find what you need in the Japanese Garden.

> *(The light shifts.)*

TOMMY Z. Not long after that, Grace stands in her house, with her suitcases beside her.

> (**KAT** *is there, too, wearing the dress that* **GRACE** *bought her – with her combat boots, but without all the other obscuring layers over it.)*

KAT. It's so far away.

GRACE. I know! I had to get a passport.

>   *(Beat.)*

Maybe I'll finally write a guidebook about a place I've actually been.

KAT. Japan?

GRACE. Cancer.

>   *(Beat.)*

A map of cancer || Strange and terrifying place || You are not alone.

KAT.   **GRACE.**
Haiku.   Haiku.

>   **(HARUKI** *steps forward, carrying his suitcase.)*

HARUKI. Ready?

>   **(GRACE** *nods, then gives her keys to* **KAT.***)*

GRACE. You have to water the plants.

KAT. I will.

GRACE. And text me every other day.

KAT. I will.

GRACE. And call Tommy if you need anything!

KAT. I will!

GRACE. And take care of yourself.

KAT. I will.

>   *(Pause.)*

Are you sure you want to do this?

GRACE. Move to Japan?

KAT. No.

GRACE. Risk loving someone?

KAT. No!

(*Beat.*)

Let me live in your house while you're gone.

GRACE. Yes. Yes, I'm absolutely sure about that.

(*Beat.*)

Now you have a place where you belong. A roof over your head. A refrigerator full of food. A job at the Japanese Garden. And time to figure out what you want to do with your life.

(**KAT** *looks unsure.*)

I'll be back in two months.

KAT. For your scan.

GRACE. Yes. And to check on you.

(**KAT** *throws her arms around* **GRACE** *and they hug.*)

(*Then she hugs* **HARUKI**, *and he hugs her back.*)

KAT. (*To* **GRACE.**) Are we going to be okay?

GRACE. I don't know.

(*A moment.*)

(*To* **HARUKI.**) Are we going to be okay?

HARUKI. I don't know.

GRACE. (*To* **KAT.**) We're going to try.

(**KAT** *looks over at* **TOMMY,** *who nods.*)

(**TOMMY** *turns to the audience.*)

TOMMY Z. And then Haruki and Grace pick up their suitcases...

KAT. ...take each other's hands...

GRACE. ...and step gently into the loud and perilous world.

(**KAT** *and* **TOMMY** *watch as* **GRACE** *and* **HARUKI** *step forward, into the world, together.*)

End of Play